Peter & Paul

Present

Ten Naughty Stories

十个淘气的故事

Learning English the Naughty Way

英语 – 中文

English – Chinese

The ten stories in this book are entirely a work of fiction. The names, characters and incidents portrayed in them are the work of the authors' imagination. Any resemblance to actual persons, living or dead, events or locations is entirely coincidental, but completely plausible.

Ten Naughty Stories
First published in Great Britain by

Leopard Publishing Ventures Ltd
Hampshire SO212PR
www.magickgate.com
magickgate@outlook.com

A CIP catalogue record is available from the British Library.

ISBN: 978-0-9574550-5-4

Dedication

For all who like naughty things

Affaires d'amour or wanton flings

Always keep an open mind

Embrace who or what you find

Acknowledgements

Peter & Paul would like to thank Ann Huan for translating the stories in this book into brilliant Chinese. They would also like to thank all the teachers they have ever known, both old or wise and young or foolish, but especially Major Watts who taught Paul the Marseillaise and "Stuffy" Stowe who used to hit him over the head with a Latin dictionary.

Contents

Foreword

Here are ten stories from our two books, Over & Under, Parts I and II. Each story comes with a postcard picture and its Chinese translation. The stories also come with notes in English to help you with jokes and cultural references. At the end of the book is a supplement with teaching ideas to use communicatively and creatively in the language classroom. We hope you enjoy our stories and learn some English along the way.

这是我们摘自我们的两本书，上面和下面，第一部和第二部中的十个淘气的故事。每个故事结合了一张明信片图片和中文翻译。这些故事也加入了英语注释来帮您理解故事中的玩笑和文化。书的最后附录有教学提示，用来在语言课上交流和创造使用。我们希望您喜欢我们的故事并且同时学习英语。

Peter & Paul

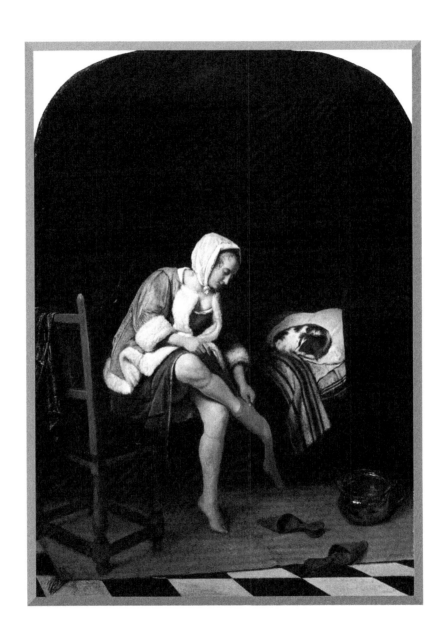

天高皇帝遠

When the cat's away, the mice will play

The Neighbour's Clogs

Sabi had been away on business in the north. When she got to Raff's place, he was out, so she phoned him on his mobile.

"Where are you, amore?"

"At the Poly.[1] - Where are you?"

"Sitting on your bed."

"With or without your undies?"

"*Porco,*[2] when are you coming home?"

Sabi hung up. As she did, she noticed a pair of *zoccoli*, or clogs, typically worn by Italians around the house, poking out from under the bed.

The *zoccoli* were old and worn. Her own *zoccoli* were pristine and new. Raff himself did not own a pair of *zoccoli*.

Sabi went out onto the landing and rang the neighbour's doorbell.

"Do these belong to you?" she said.

"I've been looking for my *zoccoli* everywhere," said the neighbour, hardly batting an eyelid.

If by now, of course, she had grown used to Raff's ways, when he came home from work and tried to put his arms around her waist, Sabi pushed him away.

They used to fight like cats and dogs. In spite of his peccadilloes, however, Sabi was still in love with Raff.

"I can't believe you did it with that *zoccola*![3] She is over fifty!"

"*Dai,*[4] Sabi," he said. "She was lonely."

Sabi shook her head and closed the bathroom door. A moment later, she came back out.

Ignoring Raff, who was lying on the bed looking miserable, Sabi went onto the landing and, for the second time that day, rang the neighbour's doorbell.

"I believe you also forgot this," she said, handing the older woman her toothbrush.

---

[1] In the Italian university system all science subjects are taught at the Polytechnic, or Poly.

[2] *Porco* means pig.

[3] *Zoccola* (feminine singular) is a prostitute, whore or hussy. It might also be translated "bitch". *Zoccoli* (masculine plural) are the typical wooden shoes worn by Italians around the house, ideal for the tiled floors of their houses and flats.

[4] An expression of exasperation, similar to "Come off it!" or "Give over!" in English.

邻居的木屐鞋

莎比去了北部出差，等她回来到拉夫的地方找他，他不在，莎比拨通了他的电话。

"你在哪儿呢，亲爱的？"

"在学校呢，你呢？"

"正坐在你的床上呢。"

"穿了内裤还是没穿？"

"猪头。你什么时候回家？"

莎比挂断电话。电话刚放下，她就发现床底下伸出来的一对木屐鞋，意大利人经常在家穿这种鞋。

这对木屐鞋又老又旧。她自己的那对是全新刚买的，而拉夫从来就不穿木屐鞋。

莎比走出楼梯口，按响了邻居的门铃。

"这是属于你的吧？"她问道。

"我到处在找我的木屐鞋。"邻居答到，眼睛都不眨一下。

莎比早已习惯拉夫的这种作风，等到他下班回家想拦腰搂住她的时候，她把他推开了。

他们曾经打起架来就像猫狗大战。可尽管拉夫有这些瑕疵，莎比仍然爱他。

"我简直无法相信你居然跟那个老妓女上床了，她都五十好几啦！"

"别这样，莎比"拉夫说道，"她当时很孤独。"

莎比摇了摇头，走进浴室里关上门，过了一小会儿她又出来了。

无视躺在床上看上去有些痛苦的拉夫，莎比径直来到楼道，第二次按响了邻居的门铃。

"我想你还忘了这个."她说着，伸手递给那个老女人她的牙刷。

一朝被蛇咬，十年怕井繩

Once bitten, twice shy

Very Bad

Jerry was indeed a handsome man, and not only that, he had whiff of rakish class about him. The devil-may-care smile, the mop of unruly but not untidy hair,[5] the loafers and the tailor made blazer with the funky[6] silk lining.

He was working his way through a whisky at the bar while wryly batting away[7] the enquiries from interested parties until a determined brunette brushed aside the competition and sat down on the stool beside him.

"I don't understand what you are doing here."

"I don't either but it always makes sense in the end."

"Can I buy you a drink?"

"Sure. But remember that I am dangerous."

"Isn't that a bit melodramatic?"

"Sure, but it is true nonetheless."

"Well, I suppose there is always a little truth in melodrama."

"One more drink and I swear you will be out of your depth."

"Oh, please! I can take care of myself."

When Jerry woke up the following morning, it took a few minutes to make sense of his surroundings. It was not his hotel, but the inside of a police cell. It made no sense and was not at all what was supposed to happen.

He went to the tiny opening in the door and shouted for someone to come.

No one came.

Thoroughly depressed, he sat down on the bed. To make matters worse, he had a hangover and was hungry.

Moments later, the door rattled as the bolt was drawn back.

In walked the brunette from last night.

"Told you I was dangerous," she said, smoothing down her uniform.

---

[5] Although messy in appearance, Jerry believes he is a rather sophisticated womaniser.
[6] Fashionable, trendy. Jerry must be very pleased with the lining of his jacket.
[7] To bat away is a metaphor from the game of cricket. Jerry is being dismissive of potential dates.

坏极了

杰瑞确实是个很好看的男人，不仅仅如此，他还有着一股放荡浪子的气质。玩世不恭的笑容，狂野又不失齐整的一头蓬松的头发，乐福鞋外加量身定做的时髦丝质料子的小西装。

他此刻正坐在吧台旁喝着威士忌同时表情冷漠地避开来自各方兴致勃勃地试探和询问，直到一位很有决心的深褐色头发女郎扫除周围障碍径自来到他身边的小凳子上坐下。

"我不明白您在这儿做什么。"

"我也是，可最终总会有那么些道理。"

"我能给您买杯酒吗？"

"当然可以，不过请记住我可是很危险的。"

"这样说不觉得有点太戏剧化吗？"

"这个嘛，我想戏剧中也总有一些真实成分的。"

"再多喝一杯的话我保证你就要醉了。"

"噢拜托，我能照顾好自己。"

当杰瑞第二天早上醒来的时候，他花了好几分钟才搞明白自己身处何处。他不在他的酒店，而是在警察局的监狱里。这不但完全没有道理也完全不是他所预计的事情发展的轨迹。

他走到门上的那个小开口旁大声呼叫引起注意。

但是没有人来。

他坐在床上感到极度的郁闷。雪上加霜的是，他宿醉未醒而且还饿极了。

过了一会儿，门栓转动，门被打开了。

走进来的是昨晚的那个深褐色女郎。

"告诉你了我很危险的" 她说道，整理了整理她的制服。

早起的鳥兒有蟲吃

The early bird catches the worm

The Emperor and Scribe

(From Tacitus,[8] lost annals)

That Tiberius had the reputation for unimaginable debauchery and licentiousness was due, in no small part, to his scribe, Lucius.

Recalled to Rome from his exile in Capri,[9] after the death of his stepfather, Augustus, who he had always disliked for his moral insincerity, the new emperor was keen to sweep everything under the carpet; among his papers were various scrolls detailing practices and habits that, well, are best left to the imagination.

"Lucius," he said, calling the scribe to his study, "I have some work for you. After you have finished burning these scrolls, I will allow you to join the revels."

Lucius, who was under no illusions as to his master's intended meaning, was prepared for such an eventuality.

"Sire," he said, "I fear I have lost the appetite for such practices."

"Do not be a spoil sport, Lucius. You must do your duty and please your master one last time."

Lucius began to stoke the fire; Tiberius returned to his official letters. "Sire," said Lucius, "I feel bound to inform you that copies of the scrolls are in the hands of a fellow scribe. In the event of my death, they will be handed to your mother, the Empress Livia."

Of all his many enemies, the new emperor feared more than any his mother.

If Lucius, however, was able to leave Capri with his life, he was not safe for long. When the emperor's mother died, at the ripe age of eighty-seven, the scribe lost his sole protector.

When Tiberius's guard knocked at the door, he was found in bed with his slave.

The scribe was put to death, but his slave was freed.

---

[8] Tacitus (56-117), chronicler of the Early Roman Empire.
[9] Emperor Tiberius (42 BC-33AD) had a villa on Capri where, prior to becoming Emperor, he was exiled. In *The Annals* Tacitus suggests that Tiberius' villa was indeed a place of unimaginable debauchery and licentiousness.

皇帝与他的记书员

（来自塔西佗，遗失的编年史）

古罗马皇帝提笔略之所以有着极度纵情酒色的名声，很大程度上要归功于他的记书员卢修斯。

提笔略十分讨厌他继父奥古斯都那道德的虚伪。当奥古斯都死后，在卡普里岛被放逐的提笔略收到召回罗马的命令。这个新皇帝急切地想要把过去的所作所为掩盖，而有关他的文章很多都是详尽描述那些各位读者可以尽情想象到的有关他各种癖好和行为的卷轴。

"卢修斯，" 他说道，把他的记书员叫到书房里， "我这儿有些工作给你，等你将这些卷轴全部都烧完的话，我就允许你加入我们的狂欢。 "卢修斯十分清楚他的主人说这话的真正意图，早已准备好了会有这样的下场。

"陛下，" 他说道： "我恐怕已经对这些乐子没什么兴趣了。"

"别这么扫兴卢修斯，你必须完成你的使命和取悦你的主人这么最后一次。"

卢修斯开始烧火，提笔略重新回到处理公务中去了， "陛下，"卢修斯说， "我感到有义务告诉你所有的这些卷轴的副本都已经在另一个记书员的手中了。如果我死了，他们将会把这些副本交到您母亲莉薇娅女皇那儿去。"

在他众多的敌人当中，我们的新皇帝最害怕的就是他的母亲。

虽然卢修斯有幸活着离开卡普里岛，他的性命并没有获得很长的保障。当皇帝的母亲在八十七岁高龄去世了以后，这位记书员丧失了他唯一的保护伞。

当提笔略的守卫敲开房门的时候，卢修斯与他的奴隶在床上被发现。

这位记书员被判处死刑，而他的奴隶则获得了自由。

自助者天助

Heaven helps those who help themselves

The Wall Flowers

One summer Laura went on a budget holiday to Spain with her girlfriend, June. As soon as they left Essex, they started drinking with some Chelsea boys[10] in the airport bar and nearly missed the plane. The holiday was a real lark.[11] June found a Chelsea shirt to take off every night, but no one, in Chelsea shirts or otherwise, appeared to be interested in Laura.

"He was nice, Lar. Why ever not?"

"He's too young, June. That's why."

"I would not have said no."

"There is always tomorrow night."

"That's what you said last night."

On the very last night of the holiday Laura dolled herself up,[12] squeezed into a pair of tight jeans and put on her red heels. She went out without any real expectations.

The bar thinned out[13] until June had gone off with Number Seven and Laura was left all on her lonesome.[14]

"Why aren't you dancing?"

"Not into it."

"Me neither. What are you into?"

Laura shrugged.

"Can I buy you a drink?"

"You a drinker then?" she said sarcastically.

"No, I am just being polite."

Laura looked up at the wall flower standing in front of her.

"Alright, what are we going to do?" she said.

"Come on," he said, taking her by the hand.

They walked for several hundred yards; then he stopped. "Wait here," he said, "while I get something from my room."

Laura sighed and lit a cigarette. I'll give him five minutes, she thought.

---

[10] The story implies that Laura and June are like characters in a reality show. Is there a Chinese equivalent of Essex girls and Chelsea boys?

[11] Great fun.

[12] To get ready to go out for the evening. A typical expression used by an Essex girl before she goes out.

[13] Become progressively empty.

[14] Profoundly alone.

He was back in three, guitar in one hand and bottle in the other. "I thought we could go to the beach," he said.

The following morning June burst into Laura's room. "Where were you last night? You get lucky then?"

"Juney," said Laura, "you cannot imagine what a night I had."

"I knew it. So what happened?"

"We sat on the beach and he sang songs to me under the silvery moon."

壁花小姐

劳拉与她的女友琼暑假的时候穷游去西班牙度假。她们刚离开艾塞克斯就在机场的酒吧里和一些很洋气的切尔西球迷喝酒还差点错过了飞机。整个假期都非常愉悦。琼基本上每晚都能找到一件切尔西球衣脱，而另一方面，似乎没有人，不管穿着切尔西球衣还是其他衣服，对劳拉感兴趣。

"他挺不错的呀，劳拉，为什么不跟他在一块儿？"

"他太年轻了琼，这就是原因。"

"我就不那么认为。"

"明晚还有机会的。"

"你昨天晚上就是这么说的。"

在她们假期的最后一晚，劳拉粉墨上场，穿上紧身牛仔裤和红色高跟鞋。她出去的并没有任何实际的期望。

酒吧里的人开始陆续离开，琼早已跟"七号"离开了，只有劳拉独自剩下。

"为什么您不跳舞呢？"

"不是太感兴趣。"

"我也不怎么感兴趣，那您对什么感兴趣呢？"

劳拉耸耸肩。

"我能给您买杯酒吗？"

"你是个酒鬼咯？" 劳拉很讽刺地说。

"不，我只是礼貌而已。"

劳拉抬头看见墙上壁花竖立在她的面前。

"好吧，我们接下来该做什么呢？" 她问道。

"跟我来，" 他说道，牵起她的手。

他们走了几百码，然后他突然停住了，"在这儿等我一下，"他说道，"等我从我房间里那点儿东西。"

劳拉轻叹了口气然后点燃了一根香烟。我最多等他五分钟，她想。

他三分钟左右就回来了，一只手里拿着吉他，另一只手里提着酒。"我想我们可以去沙滩，"他说。

第二天早上琼冲进劳拉的房间，"你昨晚儿去哪儿了？所以你跟他上床了？"

"亲爱的琼，"劳拉说道，"你无法想象我度过了一个怎样的夜晚。"

"我就知道！告诉我发生什么了。"

"我们坐在沙滩上，他在皎洁的月光下为我唱情歌。"

防人之心不可無

He that reckons without the host must reckon again

Dust and Drapery

Chevalier de Seingult[15] had a saying that an affair consisted of four acts.

The first act was like the entrée or solicitation, the second act was like a further hors d'oeuvre in anticipation of the *primo* and the *secondo*.[16] Of course, these culinary metaphors were not always appropriate.

In the case of Signorina Teresa Imer, things had never gone beyond the second act, and those appetizing hors d'oeuvres. The Chevalier had been called away from Venice for a number of years, but on his return to the city of his birth, he had the good fortune to be reacquainted with his former patron; which is why he was now wending his way, via gondola, to a masked ball at the invitation of Signor Malipiero.[17]

"All good things come to he who waits," declared the masked knight.

"If you think I am such an easy catch, you will have to wait a little longer."

So saying, the Signorina Teresa Imer managed to give the Chevalier the slip between the embonpoints of two overlaid galleys.[18]

If the Chevalier was obliged to dally during the *intermezzo*; he need not have worried. When, a little while later, he came across his little boat giggling behind the curtains in one of the upper rooms, he seized her in his embrace.

"*Aspetti, Signor,*" she said. "You would not wish to ruin my dress."

They were in one of those rooms that are often kept shut during the winter months, and there were dust everywhere.

By now feeling both gallant and impetuous, the Chevalier pulled on one of the drapes and laid it on the floor for Signorina Teresa Imer to lie on.

The Chevalier lifted the Signorina's sail and undid his own small pocket. With his customary detachment mingled with ardour, he was able to observe the climax to this most surprising of third acts.

The sighs of the Signorina were reaching a crescendo when there came a false note.

The Signorina exploded with a huge sneeze.

"I'm sorry," she said. "These drapes are full of dust!"

---

[15] Famous Italian lover, Giacomo Casanova (1725-1798). The Chevalier de Seingult was one of Casanova's many aliases.

[16] First and second courses in Italian meals.

[17] One of Casanova's Venetian patrons.

[18] Imagine Casanova squeezing between two large and big-breasted ladies, who are, in this case, the galleys.

塞恩加尔骑士曾经说过一段外遇包含四幕场景

第一个场景类似于入场或者诱惑，第二个场景则是在头盘和正餐之前的餐前小点心。当然，这些用餐比喻并不总是那么恰当。

对特蕾莎伊梅尔小姐来说，事情总是停留在第二阶段，那些餐前的小点心。塞恩加尔骑士已经被召离威尼斯好多年了，当他再次回到自己出生的这个城市时，他有幸重新被介绍给昔日的资助人，这就是为什么他正坐在小划船上，受马利皮耶罗先生的邀请去往化妆舞会的路上。

"幸运总是降临在耐心等待的人身上，"这位戴着面具的骑士如此说道。

"如果您认为我那么容易得手的话，恐怕您需要等很久了。"

这么说着，特蕾莎伊梅尔小姐成功地穿过两位体态丰腴的女士的夹缝从他身边逃走了。

如果说塞恩加尔骑士必须要在幕间剧中浪费点儿时间，他也没有什么可担心的。不一会儿，他就等到了他的时机，发现特蕾莎小姐在楼上一间房间的窗帘背后咯咯地笑，他一把将她搂入怀中。

"慢点儿，先生，"她说，"您会弄皱我的裙子的。"

他们所在的房间是那种在冬季一直紧闭的屋子，房间里布满了灰尘。

此刻骑士已充满了殷勤和冲动，他将一块儿窗帘扯下，铺在地上让特蕾莎小姐躺在上面。塞恩加尔掀起特蕾莎小姐的裙子和解开了自己的裤子，当他一贯的超然态度混合着狂热，他即将见证这最令人意外的第三幕的高潮。

特蕾莎小姐的喘息声越来越大，就在这时发出了一声异响。

特蕾莎小姐打出了一个大大的喷嚏。

"对不起，"她说，"这些窗帘上都是灰尘！"

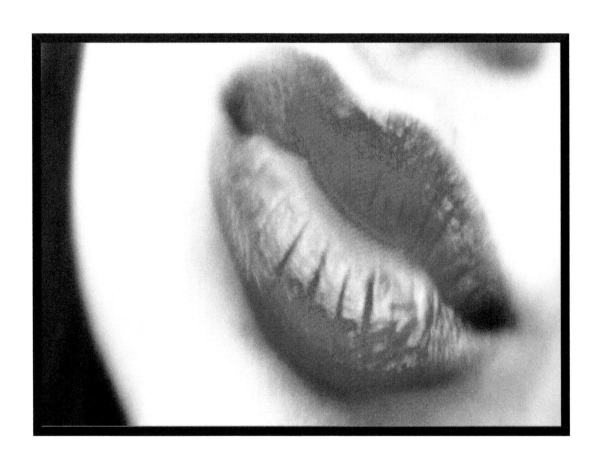

人算不如天算

To everything there is a season

Very Good

He saw her through the crowd. How unusually attractive, he thought, alone but confident, not quite part of the scene, but detached, perhaps amused by it all.

They spoke briefly. She smiled at him and they wandered outside.

"What do you do?"

"I am a writer."

"That is absurd but romantic nonetheless. I don't know any writers."

"What do you do?"

"That would be telling. But I am very good at it."

"I don't know anyone who professes to be very good at something, so that makes a first for me too."

"You know I believe it is even harder to find people like me than it is writers. What do you write about?"

"Many things. Mostly I am a storyteller in whatever form it needs."

"What form do I need?"

"Perhaps a short story?"

"How would you begin?"

"Oh, I would begin right here."

"Then what?"

"We would slip away for dinner a deux.[19] There is a good brasserie nearby that I know well."

"And what next?"

"We would stroll along the river in the starlight and watch the city go to sleep."

"When would we sleep?"

"Good question. I should finish the story first."

"Do you kiss me?"

"I have not got that far."

"That's a pity," she said.

She reached up and kissed him with lingering tenderness on the mouth.

"I told you I was very good."

Then she walked off.

---

[19] An intimate and romantic dinner for two.

专长

他在人群中看到她。"真是与众不同的吸引人"，他想，"孤独却很自信，不合主流，孤傲自赏。"

他们简单地说了几句。她对他笑笑，然后他们走了出去。

"你做什么职业的？"

"我是一个作家。"

"真荒唐，但很浪漫。我还不认识任何作家呢。"

"你做什么职业的？"

"说不准。不过我有专长。"

"我还不认识谁特别擅长某个专业，所以这对我也是第一次。"

"你知道么，我觉得找到像我这样的人比找个作家更难。你通常写什么的呀"

"很多东西。通常我写各种文风的故事。"

"我算什么文风？"

"也许一个短故事？"

"你会怎么开头？"

"啊，我会现在就开头。"

"然后呢？"

"我们溜出去吃晚餐。我知道附近有个很好的饭馆。"

"再然后呢？"

"我们在星空下漫步河畔，看着这个城市慢慢沉睡。"

"那我们什么时候睡？"

"好问题，让我先把故事讲完。"

"你会吻我吗？"

"我还没说到那段呢。"

"真可惜，" 她说。

她伸起身，吻了他，嘴唇温柔地在他的唇边逗留。

"我和你说过我有专长。"

然后她走了。

風向轉變時,有人築牆,有人造風車

One door closes… another opens

The Snake

Wang Jia was one of the Sing Sing Girls[20] living in Hebei province which at that time was run by the Zhili clique.

One day, the artist Zhang Dun came to see her. "*Baobei*," he said, "you spend too much money. I can no longer afford to keep you here."

Wang Jia would have no truck with Zhang Dun's argument. "You make me laugh," she said. "How can we afford to live when you are always away gambling with your friends?"

"It is no use," said Zhang Dun, throwing up his arms. "I will go and talk to the Zhili clique. Perhaps they will give me another chance."

Wang Jia scoffed sarcastically:

"With your book keeping skills, do you think they will listen to you?"

Sighing, Zhang Dun admitted he did not know what to do, but Wang Jia had a plan. "Send word to the Zhili clique," she said. "There will be an auction of your masterpiece. You will tell them I will be there to sing and dance for them."

On the day of the auction, the members of the Zhili clique came to the house of ill repute where they were invited to lie on hugging pillows and served *Baijiu* "vodka".

When the *guqín* player struck up, Wang Jia entered the room in her *cheongsam* dress, dancing and singing around the captivated warlords.

The music stopped; stepping forward, Zhang Dun took up a pair of scissors and cut down the seam of Wang Jia's *cheongsam* dress.

To the gasps of the Zhili clique, a bold red snake writhed on Wang Jia's back.

So it was that Zhang Dun was able to pay his debts as each man spent the night with his masterpiece.

---

[20] At the time the story is set, the 1920s. prostitutes were known as Sing Sing girls.

蛇

王佳是住在河北省的一名陪客小姐，由志力帮管。

有一天，画家张敦来找她。"宝贝"，他说，"你挥霍无度。我没法再供养你了。"

王佳不理会张敦的话。"真好笑"，她说，"是因为你总爱和你的朋友出去赌，我们才没钱的。"

"没办法了，" 张敦挥了挥手说。"我会去和志力帮商量的。也许他们会再给我个机会。"

王佳讥笑了下。

"瞧你的账本，你觉得他们会理你吗？"

张敦叹了口气，承认他也不知道怎么办，但王佳说她有个计划。"和志力帮说，"她说到，"你会搞个珍品拍卖会。你告诉他们我会在那儿为他们唱歌跳舞的。"

拍卖那天，志力帮的成员不情缘地来了，他们被邀请躺在垫子上喝白酒。

当古琴弹奏结束，王佳穿着旗袍进场，绕着着迷的帮主们又唱又跳。

音乐停了；张敦上前一步，把王佳的旗袍沿着边缘剪开。

是志力帮的人的惊讶的是，王佳的背上缠绕着一条显眼的红蛇。

张敦最终偿还了欠债，因为每个成员与他的珍品共进了良宵。

苦口良藥

Like father, like son

The Snow Child

A rich merchant by the name of Mercutio[21] was called away on business during the early winter months. When snow began to fall on the ground, the mountain pass became blocked, causing delay to Mercutio's return.

On his return Mercutio found his wife had taken to her bed.

"What is the matter, my love? Are you ailing?"

"I am with child," she said.

"How did this happen?" he asked.

"I was on my way home from the fields," she said, "when I ate a snow drop."

Pretending to believe her, Mercutio ordered the house servant to fetch some soup.

The snow child was born in the autumn.

A few years later, Mercutio was away on business when the snow began to fall. He came home to find his wife once more in bed.

"What is the matter, my love? Are you ailing?"[22]

"I am with child," she said.

Mercutio appeared satisfied.

"It is time our child saw something of the world," he said. "I will take him away for few days to the coast."

In the port, Mercutio met with a certain Greek Captain of his acquaintance who was to set sail for the Hellespont and the Sultan's palace.

"Go with this man," he said, turning to his son. "You will see the world."

The Greek Captain gave Mercutio a bag of *piastre*[23] and led the child on board his ship.

While the child was ignorant of his fate, Mercutio returned home, laden with merchandise.

His pregnant wife came to the door. "Where is our son?" she said. "What has happened to him?"

"It is hot down on the coast," said Mercutio. "He must have melted away."

---

[21] The name Mercutio is derived from the word "mercurial" meaning moody and unpredictable. Mercutio is also Romeo's friend in Shakespeare's *Romeo and Juliet* (1591-5?).
[22] Sick. Ailing is an archaic expression, as is "I am with child."
[23] Old money in Renaissance Italy (1330-1550), used by Venetian merchants.

雪娃

蒙库诺是一个富有的商人，冬季刚开始的时候他去远方做笔生意。开始下雪后，路被雪封了，蒙库诺只能延迟回家。

当他回到家他看到他的妻子睡在床上。

"亲爱的，你怎么了？生病了吗？"

"我怀孕了，" 她说。

"怎么可能？" 他问。

"我从田野间回家，" 她解释道， "我吃了一块雪。"

假装相信了她，蒙库诺让家里的仆人煮些汤给她喝。

雪娃秋天出生了。

几年后，蒙库诺又在刚开始下雪的时候去远方做生意。他回到家后再次看到他的妻子睡在床上。

"亲爱的，你怎么了？生病了吗？"

"我怀孕了，" 她说。

蒙库诺看上去很满意。

"是时候让我们的孩子看看外面的世界了，" 他说。 "我带他去海边几天。"

在港口，蒙库诺与一名过去结交的希腊船长见面，船长正准备远航去达达尼尔海峡和苏丹宫。

"跟他去，" 他转过身对他儿子说。 "你会看到外面的世界。"

希腊船长给了蒙库诺一袋钱并带着这孩子上了他的船。

那孩子还未明白他的命运，蒙库诺就已回家，揣着好多买的东西。

他的妻子来到门口。"我们的儿子呢？"她问。"他怎么了？"

"海边很热，" 蒙库诺说。 "他一定是化了。"

福無重至,禍不單行

Opportunity knocks but once

The Teapot

Jamal and Raif lugged the huge item back to the shop.

"What in heaven's name have you got there?" asked their father.

"A giant teapot!" they exclaimed proudly.

"Why?" said their father.

"We had to buy it – it is so cool!" answered Jamal.

"Oh really?" said his father. "How much?"

"Um...."

"HOW much?"

"Six hundred."

"Do you boys actually study Maths at school?"

"Yes father, we know. It's a lot of money."

"Exactly."

"Look father, it's a friendly pot."

"You may think so. I am wondering if a robber broke into our shop, how he might take less money than that."

"We promise we'll make it worthwhile!"

The teapot stood mournfully outside the shop for the next few weeks as Jamal and Raif worked out what to do.

Then, early one morning, they dragged another huge box into the shop.

"Oh, my, what have we here?" said their father.

"This, father, is how we are going to make our name and recover the money."

The boys unpacked the box which was filled with miniature copies of the giant teapot.

Soon a French lady came in.

"I love your giant teapot," she said, "Can I buy one of the small ones?"

The boys smiled.

Their father shrugged. As he turned round, he was also smiling.

茶壶

杰曼和莱杰把一个巨型物拖进了店里。

"天那你们带来了什么？" 他们的父亲问。

"一个巨大的茶壶！" 他们自豪地说。

"为什么？" 他们地父亲问。

"我们不得不买下它 - 它太酷了！" 杰曼回答。

"喔是吗？" 他的父亲说。"多少钱？"

"额。。。"

"到底多少？"

"600。"

"你们在学校是不是真学过数学？"

"是的父亲，我们知道，这是很大一笔钱。"

"完全正确。"

"看父亲，这是一个友好的壶？"

"你也许这么想。我怀疑若一个劫匪闯进我们的店，他是否觉得它值那么多。"

"我们保证，我们会让它值钱的！"

这个茶壶可悲地在接下去的几个星期杵在店外，而杰曼和莱杰想到底该怎么做。

然后，有一天清晨，他们又把另一个巨大的盒子拖进了店里。

"喔天那，你们又拿来了什么？" 他们的父亲问。

"这个嘛，父亲，将打响我们的名气，让我们收回成本。"

这两个男孩开始拆盒子，里面装满了那个大茶壶的克隆迷你小茶壶。

马上一个法国女子进了店。

"我很爱你们的大茶壶，" 她说， "我能买个小的吗？"

那两个男孩笑了。

他们的父亲耸耸肩。他转过身，也笑了。

酒发心腹之言

In vino veritas

A Liar and a Thief

Writers' conferences always brought out the most bookish of folk, reflected Axel. Then he bumped into Lulu.

They chatted genially about Gunter Grass[24] and blogging, Georg Pabst[25] and, funnily enough, Jonathan Livingston Seagull,[26] when she dropped the unexpected.

"Thing is, my father was a donor. I was brought up by two women." A throw-away line, but too good to miss.

Lulu described her painful upbringing, the teasing at school, "They called me the Lesbisch.[27] I hated it. I wanted to commit suicide."

It took several glasses of wine and dinner before she had finished. Axel listened carefully. When he got to the hotel, he broke out his laptop and tapped out every detail. It was the character he was missing from his novel.

The novel was in the bestseller charts; the following year, he was invited back to speak at the writers' conference.

"I doubt she'll show," he thought. But show she did and was waiting for him outside after his keynote.

"You're a bloody thief!"

"It is not exactly your story."

"You know it is."

"All right, I took it and changed it. So what?"

A curious thing happened. She stepped back and smiled.

"Well, if you are a Thief, then I am a Liar."

Axel was bemused.

"I made it up. Every word. None of it is true."

"What? You must be joking?"

"Not at all, she said. "My father worked in the Post Office and my mother was a housewife. Later on she worked for the Red Cross. I had a completely normal upbringing in the suburbs of Bonn."

Axel was so deflated he just stood there. Lulu reached up and kissed him on the cheek.

"Never mind, *mein pet*, once a thief always a thief."

Axel did not have long to reflect; when he got to the bar, his wallet was missing from his jacket pocket. He looked for her at the conference the following day but she was nowhere to be found.

---

[24] Gunter Grass (1927-2015), German writer who won the Nobel Prize for Literature in 1999.
[25] Georg Pabst (1885-1965), Austrian film director of *Pandora's Box* (1929).
[26] *Jonathan Livingston Seagull* (1970), a fable by Richard Bach (1936-).
[27] Lesbian. To English ears there would also be a pun on "bitch".

骗子和小偷

作家们的会仪总会让人觉得呆板，艾克丝想。然后他碰到了露露。

他们友好地闲聊了作家哥特格拉丝和部落格，导演乔治帕斯特和乔纳森来福敦的寓言故事海鸥，然后她突然停了下来。

"事实上，我的父亲是一个精子捐赠者。我由两个女人抚养长大。" 一个题外话，但不能错过。

露露讲述了她痛苦的成长过程，在学校被嘲笑，"他们叫我婊子。我恨死了。我当时想自杀。"

几杯葡萄酒和晚饭后她讲完了。艾克丝一直都认真地听着。

当他回到宾馆，他打开电脑写下来每个细节。这正是他小说需要的主角。

他的小说成了畅销书；第二年，他被邀请去那个作家会议演讲。

"我觉得她不会来的，" 他想到。但是她不但来了还在他的演讲后在外面等着他。

"你他妈的小偷！"

"我写的并不完全是你的故事。"

"你知道是。"

"好吧，我拿了故事然后改了下。那又怎样？"

有趣的事发生了。她后退一步笑了。

"好吧，如果你是小偷，那我就是骗子。"

艾克丝感兴趣了。

"我编造了故事。每个字。没句是真的。"

"什么？你在开玩笑？"

"没有，" 她说。 "我的父亲在邮局工作，母亲是个家庭主妇。后来她为红十字工作。我在伯恩郊区完全普通的环境下长大。"

艾克丝太失望了，他僵在了那。露露上前在他脸颊亲了下。

"没事，我亲爱的，小偷当了一次就永远是小偷。"

艾克丝不需要很久去想这话的意思；当他去了酒吧，他衣服口袋里的钱包找不到了。他第二天在会议上找她但她已经走了。

FINIS

How to use this book in a language classroom

The ideas in this supplement follow a communicative approach to language teaching, training and learning where the emphasis is on personalizing activities, integrating skills and dealing with aspects of grammar, pronunciation and vocabulary as they occur. While there are no hard and fast rules in language teaching, in my experience an eclectic approach has always seemed to work best. Following the EFL tradition, I have set the activities out as though they were lessons in stone. They are not. Please take them in the spirit they were meant and do what you like, need or want with them. What matters is progress, not perfection.

師傅領進門，修行在個人

You can lead a horse to the water,

but you cannot make it drink

ONE: Dedication Poem

ACTIVITY
Writing a short poem

LEVEL
Elementary +

TIME
45-60 min

LANGUAGE
Imperative form, word order

VOCABULARY
General

FOUR SKILLS
All

MATERIALS
Worksheet 1

RATIONALE
This activity helps students understand and appreciate a poem as well as give pleasure and satisfaction in writing their own poems in the target language.

RULE OF THUMB
Look to practice two skills per lesson.

PROCEDURE
(1)   Cut up the poem for students to order. With lower levels the teacher may choose to give the poem in bigger chunks.
(2)   Hand out the word list to order into rhyming words (Worksheet 1).
(3)   Using the rhyming words to help them order the cut up text, students are now in a position to memorise and recite the poem.

FOLLOW-UP
Students create their own short poems using their own lists of rhyming words and take a vote on the best 4-line poems in the class.

As English is a stress-based language, an additional step could involve remedial work on sentence stress. There are four beats per line (stressed syllable in bold):

    For **all** those who **like naughty things**
    Affaires d'amour and **wanton flings**

TWO: The Neighbour's Clogs

ACTIVITY
Skimming and scanning the text

LEVEL
Pre-intermediate+

TIME
45-60 min

LANGUAGE
Past tenses, reported and direct speech, possessive "s"

VOCABULARY
Household objects, rooms, relationships

FOUR SKILLS
Reading and writing

MATERIALS
Worksheet 2

RATIONALE
Promoting skimming and scanning techniques ensures students are not overwhelmed by phrases and expressions they do not initially understand in texts.

RULE OF THUMB
Good habits make good learners.

PROCEDURE
(1)　Pre-reading: elicit the keyword in the title (clogs) from the picture and write a "diamond" of other keywords from the story on the blackboard. Students can use bilingual, phone dictionaries or monolingual dictionaries to help them with new words.
(2)　While reading: students skim the text for gist meaning and scan for specific information and details (Worksheet 2). It may be a good idea to set a time limit for these exercises (1 minute per question).
(3)　After reading: students can devise their own skim or scan questions about the text.

FOLLOW-UP
On cards students write one true and two false definitions of new words. In a later lesson they can play a true or false game with the definition cards

THREE: Very Bad

ACTIVITY
What happens next?

LEVEL
Pre-intermediate+

TIME
45 min

LANGUAGE
Past tenses, comparatives and superlatives

VOCABULARY
Relationships

FOUR SKILLS
Reading and writing

MATERIALS
Worksheet 3

RATIONALE
Students use their imaginations to personalise the middle of the story and make it their own.

RULE OF THUMB
Encourage self-correction.

PROCEDURE
(1)   Hand out the beginning and end of "Very Bad" with the middle blanked out. Explain to the students they have to create the middle of the story themselves.
(2)   After exchanging their ideas, students write up their stories and post them around the room.
(3)   Students compare their story with the original "Very Bad".

FOLLOW-UP
Students can be trained to look for specific mistakes in their texts, such as word order or spelling. They can record the results on the work sheet provided and discuss which mistakes they would like to avoid in future (Worksheet 3).

As an alternative you can give students the beginning and middle of the story and students can make up the end.

FOUR: The Emperor and the Scribe

ACTIVITY
Filling in the gaps

LEVEL
Intermediate+

TIME
30 min

LANGUAGE
Past tenses, prefixes (*un-*) and suffixes (*-ness*)

VOCABULARY
Adjectives of character, family

FOUR SKILLS
Reading and writing

MATERIALS
Worksheet 4

RATIONALE
A cloze test can be useful way to test students' progress as well as prepare students for external exams. In a traditional cloze every seventh word is deleted, but you may choose to cloze only specific grammar words i.e. adjectives, verbs or nouns, depending on what your students have recently practised.

RULE OF THUMB
Encourage collaboration over competition.

PROCEDURE
(1) Dictate the cloze words in a random list of words. Alternatively, students can brainstorm words associated with the title while you feed your suggestions into their lists (Worksheet 4).
(2) Students fill in the gaps and compare their results with another pair.

FOLLOW-UP: if students are studying for exams, they can create their own cloze tests with recently learnt idioms a/o structures.

As an extra challenge, you can dictate some or all of the cloze text. While you dictate, you can clap your hands or say "blank" for the gaps in the story.

FIVE: The Wallflowers

ACTIVITY
Retelling a love story

LEVEL
Elementary+

TIME
45 min

LANGUAGE
Past tenses, reported speech

VOCABULARY
Relationships, holidays

FOUR SKILLS
All

MATERIALS
Worksheet 5 (for the teacher)

RATIONALE
Personalising and retelling a story in their own words empowers students and incentivizes their learning.

RULE OF THUMB
Keep your aims realistic and achievable for the whole class.

PROCEDURE
(1) For homework students read both English and Chinese versions of "The Wallflowers" and make a note of 5-7 words they want to remember.
(2) In class students "mumble" their recollection of the story using your blackboard cues (Worksheet 5).
(3) Students act out or role play the story in small groups, taking it in turns to be the narrator and the characters in the story.

FOLLOW-UP
Students write up their versions of the story and display the results around the room. It is a good idea to give a word limit for the story.

You may choose to put in an additional step by doing some remedial work on linking words or past tenses, or other recently practised structures and word fields.

SIX: Dust and Drapery

ACTIVITY
Telling a story with a game (Consequences)

LEVEL
Pre-intermediate+

TIME
45-60 min

LANGUAGE
He/she's got, she's wearing, past simple and continuous

VOCABULARY
Adjectives of appearance and character, clothes

FOUR SKILLS
All

MATERIALS
Worksheet 6, paper and pens

RATIONALE
This activity uses a well-known game to encourage students' creativity.

RULE OF THUMB
Personalise and make activities relevant to student needs.

PROCEDURE
(1) Brainstorm famous lovers (Casanova), poets (Dante), couples (Romeo and Juliet), beauties (Cleopatra) and beasts (Frankenstein's monster).
(2) Put the students in a circle and make sure they all have paper and pens.
(3) Dictate the instructions for the Consequences Game from Worksheet 6. After each instruction students fold their paper and pass it on.
(4) Get the students to post the stories around the room for all to see and comment upon.

FOLLOW UP
Students can write up their favourite stories and add details or recently learnt words or idioms in another class or for homework. Then they can compare their own stories with Peter & Paul's "Dust and Drapery".

SEVEN: Very Good

ACTIVITY
What are you good at?
Questionnaire

LEVEL
Beginner+

TIME
30-45 min

LANGUAGE
Question forms, *good/bad at* +ing form, *can, can't* (+ infin.)

VOCABULARY
Sports, school subjects, abilities

FOUR SKILLS
All

MATERIALS
Worksheet 7

RATIONALE
This activity is both a controlled and empowering way to activate students' question forming skills and deal with the tricky inversion of English question forms.

RULE OF THUMB
Creative questions lead to creative "chat time".

PROCEDURE
(1)   Divide the board into three columns: *very good, good, bad*, and suggests things you are good or bad at.
(2)   Get students to create their own columns with lists and share their ideas.
(3)   Model the question form and get students to practise the structure using prompts from the board.
(4)   Students devise their own questionnaires around the structure. Try to encourage students to make longer and more creative questions and integrate recently learnt structures (Worksheet 7).

FOLLOW-UP: students can text questions to friends in other classes. For homework they can write up what they find out about each other from the questionnaire.

EIGHT: The Snake

ACTIVITY
Exploring borrowed words

LEVEL
Beginner +

TIME
30-45 min

LANGUAGE
Present simple, comparatives and superlatives

VOCABULARY
Chinese words in English (e.g. *Cheongsam*)

FOUR SKILLS
Reading and writing

MATERIALS
Worksheet 8

RATIONALE
This activity sensitizes students to the relationship between their own language and the target language.

RULE OF THUMB
Exploit your students' mother tongue.

PROCEDURE
(1)   Point out the Chinese words used in the English version of "The Snake" and invite students to think of other English words borrowed from Chinese.
(2)   Dictate the list of borrowed words in their own language; then get students to decide on their English spelling.
(3)   Students can check and match definitions of borrowed words against the answers to Worksheet 8.

FOLLOW-UP
Students decide on their favourite borrowed words and design a small poster to illustrate their meaning.

NINE: The Snow Child

ACTIVITY
Expand a "telegram" folk story

LEVEL
Pre-intermediate+

TIME
45-60 min

LANGUAGE
Past tenses, passive form, infinitive of purpose, articles

VOCABULARY
Borrowed words (from Italian), weather and travel

FOUR SKILLS
All

MATERIALS
Worksheet 9

RATIONALE
This activity uses cognitive skills and knowledge of grammar rules to sensitize students to build on a telegram version of a folk story. In the telegram version of the story only the content words such as nouns and verbs are given. Non-content words such as auxiliary verbs, articles and prepositions are deleted.

RULE OF THUMB
Exploit your student's general knowledge.

PROCEDURE
(1) Elicit ideas on how to expand the example sentence in the telegram story into a more complete sentence (Worksheet 9).
(2) Students work on expanding the rest of the telegram and check their versions against another pair's.
(3) Invite students to compare their stories with the original "Snow Child".

FOLLOW-UP
Tell students "The Snow Child" is based on a well-known European folk story. Students can brainstorm folk stories from their own language and write their own telegram stories for other pairs or groups to expand.

TEN: The Teapot

ACTIVITY
Pronunciation of –ed endings

LEVEL
Pre-intermediate+

TIME
30 min

LANGUAGE
Past tenses, adverbs

VOCABULARY
Regular verbs, reporting verbs

FOUR SKILLS
Listening and speaking

MATERIALS
Worksheet 10

RATIONALE
This activity sensitizes students to the pronunciation of –ed endings.

RULE OF THUMB
Be descriptive, not proscriptive.

PROCEDURE
(1)   Write three columns on the blackboard $/t/$, $/d/$, $/id/$. Invite students to categorize regular verbs according to the sound of the –ed ending.
(2)   Get students to decide which column verbs from the story belong to (Worksheet 10).
(3)   Students think of other regular verbs and add them to respective columns.

FOLLOW-UP
Students can create their own sound discrimination exercise. E.g. Which is the odd one out? - work**ed**, promis**ed**, unpack**ed**, dragg**ed** (Answer: dragg**ed**).

If you wish, you can give the rules for –ed pronunciation. $/id/$ follows $/t/$ and $/d/$ in verb endings. The difference between $/t/$ and $/d/$ endings is small. $/t/$ comes after a voiced consonant and $/d/$ after an unvoiced consonant. If your students are confused by the difference, they can try blocking their ears and saying the base form of the verb aloud to decide whether the final consonant is said with or without voice.

ELEVEN: A Liar and a Thief (1)

ACTIVITY
Describing a face

LEVEL
Beginner+

TIME
45-60 min

LANGUAGE
He/she's got,
present continuous

VOCABULARY
Adjectives of description, character

FOUR SKILLS
Listening and speaking

MATERIALS
Worksheet 11 (optional), photos of famous people

RATIONALE
This activity is a humorous way to develop speaking skills at lower levels and gives confidence to students facing internal and external exams.

RULE OF THUMB
Create lessons for different learning styles.

PROCEDURE
(1)   Use the picture from "A Liar and a Thief" to elicit and model the target structure.
(2)   Students take it in turns to describe the man in the picture with further picture prompts from the board a/o using a substitution drill.
(3)   Brainstorm further ideas for describing each other.
(4)   Elicit the names of famous people from photos and add students' own suggestions.
(5)   Divide the class into two teams who take it in turns to guess which famous person is being described.

FOLLOW-UP
Students create a short description of the liar and the thief against a background of their choice or one chosen by you. They dictate the description to another pair who draw what they hear.

TWELVE: A Liar and a Thief (2)

ACTIVITY
Planning your own lesson

LEVEL
(Beginner +)

TIME
(45 mins)

LANGUAGE
(Present Simple,
adverbs of frequency)

VOCABULARY
(Routines)

FOUR SKILLS
(Listening and speaking)

MATERIALS
Worksheet 12

RATIONALE
Devising your own lesson from materials in a resource book can free you up and make you realise the limitations of a particular approach or course book you have been using.

RULE OF THUMB
An eclectic approach works best.

PROCEDURE
(1) Use Worksheet 12 to help you devise a lesson plan from the materials provided in *Ten Naughty Stories*.
(2) Talk through your lesson plan with another teacher.
(3) Get your colleague to observe your lesson and give feedback.

FEEDBACK
It is very easy to be overly critical. Focus on the positive in the lesson. Suggest one, at most two things to work on for next time.

Worksheets

Worksheet 1: Rhyming words

Match the words that rhyme: e.g. **tart-heart**

Naughty-love; love-behind; thing-cream; mind-dove; skirt-fleas; dream-fling; chin-hat; keys–shirt; affair-feet; flat-shin; **tart-heart**; meat-share

Add more examples to your list: (?)–(?); (?)-(?); (?)–(?)

Worksheet 2: Skimming and scanning

Skimming	Scanning
1. Who is Raff?	1. Where is Sabi at the start of the story?
2. What does Sabi find in Raff's room?	2. What does Raff do when he sees Sabi?
3. Is Sabi happy to see Raff?	3. What is the difference between Raff's clogs and the clogs Sabi finds?
4. Who is lonely?	4. Why do Sabi and Raff fight like cats and dogs?
5. What does Sabi find in Raff's bathroom?	5. How many times does Sabi ring the neighbour's doorbell?
Add some more questions of your own.	

Worksheet 3: Noticing Mistakes

SP = Spelling; GR=Grammar; WO=Word Order; WW=Wrong Word; T=Tense; P=Punctuation; ∧ = Missing Word

SP	
GR	
WO	
WW	
T	
P	
∧	

Worksheet 4: Cloze Exercise

Use the words to fill the blanks in the text: **left – among - no - unimaginable – keen - recalled – in – who - moral – practices.**

That Tiberius had the reputation for (1) _____debauchery and licentiousness was due, in (2) _____small part, to his scribe, Lucius.
(3) _____to Rome from his exile (4) _____Capri, after the death of his stepfather, Augustus, (5) _____ he had always disliked for his (6) _____insincerity, the new emperor was (7) _____ to sweep everything under the carpet; (8) _____ his papers were various scrolls detailing (9) _____ and habits that, well, are best (10) _____ to the imagination.

Worksheet 5: Teacher's Board

A clear and meaningful board is a handy way to cue your activities and jog student's memories.

(Cues)	(Lesson Title: The Wallflowers)	-ing
-ed miss /t/ sigh /d/ start /id/	**(Working Space)** lonesome (alONE) heels guitAR bot(t)l(e) b/i:/ch bar	drink smok(e) lov(e) dream kiss eat
IR	song	- er
go sit put sing	**(New Structure)** Are you INt(e)rest/id/ in DANCing? Yes, I am. No, I am not.	

1. Can you interpret my board? What might have been taught in this lesson?
2. Can you interpret the working space in the middle of the board?
3. Can you interpret the new structure space at the bottom of the board?
4. What about the left hand side of the board under cues?
5. And the right hand side of the board under the -er suffix?

Worksheet 6: Consequences Game

Write the name of a (famous) man
---(Fold)---

Write the name of a (famous) woman
---(Fold)---

Write three adjectives to describe him
---(Fold)---

Write three adjectives to describe her
---(Fold)---

Describe what he is wearing
---(Fold)---

Describe what she is wearing
---(Fold)---

Where do they go/meet?
---(Fold)---

What does he say to her?
---(Fold)---

What does she say to him?
---(Fold)---

What happens in the end?
---(Fold)---

Worksheet 7: Very Good Questionnaire

(1) Are you quite good at tennis or brilliant at it?	
(2) Are you a good kisser or a better hugger?	
(3) If you are good at tennis, are you also good at badminton?	
(4) When you were at school, were you good at maths?	
(5) If you were good at maths, are you still good at it?	
Add (7) more questions.	
Dictate 4 of your favourite questions to a member of the class.	

Worksheet 8: English words borrowed from Chinese

Can you match the English word to its definition?

Example: **char –tea (colloquial)**

Cantonese/Mandarin	English	Definition (mixed up)
茶	char	toast when raising glass
長衫	cheongsam	hot drink
"請，請!"	chin chin	utensil for eating
Chop chop (pidgin)	chopstick	long clothes
炒	chow	great nobleman
風水	fengshui	food
工合	gungho	Stir fry sauce
茄汁	ketchup	tea (colloquial)
茄汁	kowtow	way of life, philosophy
功夫	kung fu	tomato sauce
荔枝	lychee	aesthetic object or scene
將軍	shogun	ready for a fight
醬油	soy	type of fruit
茶 (Amoy)	tea	general, leader
豆腐	tofu	great storm
大君	tycoon	pan or cauldron
颱風	typhoon	bean curd
颱風	wok	craving, addiction
癮	yen	bow to superior
禪	Zen	martial art

Worksheet 9: Snow Child Telegram

Expand each telegram to make a complete sentence and put the verb in brackets in an appropriate form. E.g. **Rich merchant (call) Mercutio (go) away business**
A rich merchant called Mercutio went away on business.

(1) Rich merchant (call) Mercutio (go) away business
(2) Snow (begin) fall mountain pass (block)
(3) Mercutio (return) home (find) wife bed with child
(4) I (eat) snow drop she (say)
(5) Child (be born) autumn
(6) Later Mercutio (take) son (see) port and (meet) Greek captain
(7) Captain (take) boy on board ship; now you (see) world son
(8) Mercutio (return) home wife
(9) Where (be) son she (ask)
(10) It (be) hot on coast Mercutio (say) he (melt) away

Worksheet 10: ed-endings

Put the regular verbs from the story in the correct column: **lugged, answered, asked, exclaimed, worked, promised, packed/unpacked, smiled, dragged, filled, shrugged, turned (round)**

/t/	/d/	/id/
asked	filled	visited

Worksheet 11: Picture Dictation

"The famous liar and thief, Toad is standing on a beach. He's got a false beard and a pair of glasses. Of course, he has also got a very long nose, and he is wearing a pair of colourful Bermuda shorts. Behind him two children are making a sandcastle. On his left a woman is lying on a sun-bed. She is wearing a straw hat… Toad likes the straw hat. He walks up to her and sits down in the sand. What will Toad do next?"

Worksheet 11: Lesson Plan Checklist

Is all the language in the text appropriate for the level and age group you are teaching? If not, what do you need to modify?	
Have you thought of a lead-in?	
Is there enough variety in your lesson?	
Will the students be able to follow all the stages in your lesson?	
Have you thought about skimming and scanning exercises?	
How will you deal with idioms and cultural references?	
What about follow-up activities? Homework?	
Will students be using more than one skill in your lesson?	
Is the lesson coherent and clearly signposted?	
Have you thought about the timing of your activities?	
Are the activities personalised and relevant to the students' needs?	
Is there a good balance of pair and group work in your lesson?	
☺ Add (2) more questions to your checklist.	

Peter's Crib Sheet

Worksheet 1: Naughty-warty; love-dove; thing-fling; mind-behind; skirt-shirt; dream-cream; chin-sin; keys–fleas; affair-share; flat-hat; tart-heart; meat-feet.

Worksheet 2: Possible answers

1. Sabi's boyfriend	1. In the north
2. A pair of zoccoli or clogs.	2. Raff's clogs are old and these are new
3. Not really.	3. He tries to hug her but Sabi isn't interested.
4. Raff's neighbour.	4. Sabi is in love with Raff, but Raff wants his freedom.
5. The neighbour's toothbrush.	5. Twice.

Worksheet 4: See the story on Page 11.

Worksheet 5:

1. In this lesson the teacher has got students to retell the story called the Wallflowers in their own words.
2. The teacher has placed a word diamond on the board to cue words she wishes students to use as they tell the story. She has given a synonym for the adjective "lonesome" which appears in the story. She has drawn attention to the stressed syllable in gui**tar** and a**lone,** the silent letters in bot(t)l(e) and the long vowel sound /i:/ in beach.
3. The teacher has introduced a new structure "to be interested in something or do + ing". Highlighting of stressed syllables suggests the structure has been drilled, both chorally and individually.
4. In previous lessons students have worked on past simple forms of both regular and irregular verbs. The teacher has also drawn attention to the pronunciation of –ed endings.
5. The teacher has used cues to show base form of verbs can form gerunds ending –ing (dance – dancing) and nouns ending in –er (dance – dancer). The next lesson may involve recycling these forms.

Worksheet 8: char – tea (colloquial); cheongsam – long clothes; chin chin – toast when raising glass; chopstick – utensil for eating; chow – food; fengshui – aesthetic object or scene; gungho – ready for a fight; ketchup – tomato sauce; kowtow – bow to superior; kung fu – martial art; lychee – type of fruit; shogun – general, leader; soy – stir fry sauce; tea – hot drink; tofu – bean curd; tycoon – great nobleman; typhoon – great storm; wok – pan or cauldron; yen – craving, addiction; Zen – way of life, philosophy.

Worksheet 9: A possible solution

(1) A rich merchant called Mercutio went away on business. (2) Snow began to fall and the mountain pass was blocked. (3) Mercutio returned home to find his wife in bed with child. (4) "I ate a snow drop," she said. (5) The child was born in the autumn. (6) Later Mercutio took his son to see the port and meet a Greek captain. (7) The Greek Captain took the boy on board his ship. "Now you can see the world, my son." (8) Mercutio returned home to his wife. (9) "Where is our son?" she asked. (10) "It was hot on the coast," Mercutio said. "He melted away."

Worksheet 10

/t/	/d/	/id/
asked worked promised packed/ unpacked	filled lugged answered exclaimed smiled dragged shrugged turned (round)	(no example in story) visited divided melted (away) lasted

孔子谚语无论你走到哪里，去与所有你的心脏

Wherever you go, go with all your heart

Confucius

Glossary of EFL Terms

Though by no means an exhaustive list of EFL terms, Paul hopes the glossary helps you explore the teaching ideas in this supplement.

Aims: what the teacher hopes to achieve in the lesson both for herself and the students. For example, in a lesson involving the past simple, the teacher presents the form of regular past simple and gets students to talk about their schooldays using regular past simple forms. She might also have a personal aim: to give clearer and simpler instructions.

Brainstorming: students are put into pairs or groups to think of as many ideas, words or questions round a category or theme: for example, words linked to clothes.

Chat Time: a stage in the lesson devoted to "chatting" in the target language.

Class Profile: includes the level, age, and background of the students and what has been studied in previous lessons.

Cloze Test: a test in which traditionally every seventh word is blanked out in a text.

Communicative Approach: where the emphasis is on interaction as the means and ultimate goal of learning a language, and where fluency is encouraged over accuracy and meaning over structure.

Drilling: the target structure is modelled by the teacher and repeated by the class as a choral drill and then individually.

Eliciting: the teacher elicits an oral response from the class often with nonverbal cues by miming, for example, a word for the students to guess, or drawing a picture of the word on the blackboard.

External Exams: internationally recognised exams such as PET (Preliminary English Test), FCE (First Certificate Examination) and TOEFL (Test of English as a Foreign Language).

Follow-up Activity: an activity that exploits new language and gets students to use it productively.

Four Skills: listening, speaking, reading and writing. The four skills are divided into productive skills, speaking and writing, and receptive skills, listening and reading.

Feedback: a stage in the lesson when the teacher involves and leads the whole class in response to an activity or task.

Function: language is seen according to its function in communication. For example, when the students tell or re-tell a story, or compare one type of story with another.

Information Gap: an exercise where one student has information the other student wants, and vice versa. (See Very Good Questionnaire, Worksheet 7).

Integrating skills: an approach that looks to integrate skills within a lesson; for example, a reading lesson may also have elements of speaking i.e. discussing the text, or writing i.e. making sentences from words introduced in the text.

Lead-in: an activity that prepares the ground for the main focus of the lesson; such as using a picture to stimulate interest in a text.

Lexical Field: a series of linked vocabulary items: for example, food and drink.

Objective: what the teacher hopes the students will take away from the lesson: for example, writing a postcard story in the target language.

Pair-work/group-work: students work collaboratively on an activity or task set by the teacher.

Personalisation: the teacher adapts an exercise or activity in a course book or resource book according to the needs of the students and the classroom dynamic.

Picture dictation: the students draw what the teacher or another student describes. The standard procedure is for the person dictating to describe the scene as a whole, then a second or third time in meaningful phrase long, or sentence long bites.

Prescription v Description: in a communicative language classroom it is considered good practice to describe as opposed to prescribe rules. Example of prescription: have is an auxiliary verb. Example of description: Have is an auxiliary verb in the sentence *I have* *been to Beijing twice*, but it can also mean "to possess" as in the sentence *I have two brothers, a sister and a dog called Deng.*

Practice: the students practice the language in a meaningful way using a variety of techniques such as role play, information gap and questionnaire. (See worksheet 7).

Procedure: the steps taken by the teacher to put her lesson into practice.

Product: the material output of an activity: for example, in a writing lesson, a postcard to be sent to a friend abroad.

Production: the target structure is used in the freest possible way to exploit students' wider skills in the target language.

Recycling: the teacher re-introduces previously taught grammar or vocabulary into the practice or productive stage of the lesson.

Role Play: students take on the role of characters in a scene and act out the scene: for example, a customer and a waiter in a restaurant, or a first date (See The Wallflowers).

Skimming: students read for gist or general meaning. For example: who is the text about?).

Scanning: students scan for specific information in a text. For example: what does the word in line 7 mean? (a) ----- (b) ----- (c) ----- (d) -----

Signposting: giving clear indications to the students about what is being practised in the lesson; for example, giving the lesson a title. (See Worksheet 5).

Stage: part of the procedure of a lesson. Example: Stage (1) Brainstorm clothes words Stage (2) Exchange list with another pair or group.

Sentence stress: the stressed syllables over a whole sentence. (See Worksheet 1).

Student needs: what the students need to know in any given lesson or during a course in relation to a programme or syllabus.

Target structure: a grammatical structure that stands for the focus of the lesson: for example, in a lesson involving the irregular past simple: *Yesterday Shen went to the seaside. He didn't go to the ice cream shop, but he swam in the sea with the dolphins.*

Task: an activity set by the teacher for the students to complete. It usually involves a product. For example, work with your partner to think of ten words beginning with "s". You have (5 minutes). Find at least (20) words.

Timing: how much time the teacher allocates for an activity.

Warmer: a short five-minute activity that literally warms the students up and puts them in the mood for the lesson; for example, a word game like hangman.

Word Diamond: words from a text are placed on the black board in the shape of diamond. (See Worksheet 5).

Word Stress: a word is divided into its stressed syllables. For teaching purposes, the stressed syllable is usually marked by ■ or an accent. (See Worksheet 5).

EFL 课堂用语词汇表

虽然这份词汇表不能详尽罗列所有 EFL 课堂用语，保罗希望能以此为补充，帮助你了解 EFL 的教学理念。

Aims（目标）：老师在课堂上想要学生和自己达到的目的。例如，在介绍过去时的一节课上，老师在列出普通过去式的变换形式后让学生们用过去时讨论各自的学习生活。她或许还有一个自己的目标，更简单明了的指导学生。

Brainstorming （头脑风暴）：学生们以两人或多人小组讨论的形式围绕一个类别或主体思考出尽可能多的想法，单词或问题。例如，与服装有关的单词。

Chat time（讨论时间）：课堂上使用目标语言"讨论"的阶段。

Class profile（课堂简历）：包括学生的级别，年龄，背景资料和过去课中学到的知识点。

Cloze Test（完形填空测试）：一段文字中通常每第七个单词被空出需要填写的测试。

Communicative approach（交际教学法）：以交流为途径和最终目的学习语言方法。这种方法鼓励运用流利的语言表达出自己的意思，而不是将重点放在准确性和语法结构上。

Drilling（演练）：先由老师使用目标语法结构造句，学生集体重复，再单独重复的练习方法。

Eliciting（引申）：老师用比划的方式引出学生的口头回答。例如，通过比划或在黑板上画画的方式让学生猜单词。

External exams（外部考试）：国际认可的英语语言考试，如 PET（初级英语测试），FCE（第一英语证书考试）和 TOEFL（托福）。

Follow-up activity（跟进活动）：让学生高效地使用新学的语言知识的活动。

Four skills（四项技能）：听，说，读和写。这四项技能可以分为表达技能（说与写）和接受技能（听与读）。

Feedback（反馈）：一节课中老师参与并带领全班一起完成一项活动或任务的阶段。

Function（功能）：语言会根据它在交流中的功能被理解。例如，当学生讲述或复述一个故事，比较这类故事与其他类故事时。

Information gap（信息隔阂）：一个学生掌握其他学生想要的信息或其他学生掌握这个学生想要的信息的一种练习方式。（见表 7，很好的问卷调查）

Integrating skills（技能整合）：一种以整合四项技能为目的的教学方法。例如，阅读课中会包含说（讨论这篇文章）与写（使用文中的单词造句）的技能。

Lead-in（导入）：为一节课的学习重点作铺垫的活动。例如，用一张图片来引发学生对一篇文章的兴趣。

Lexical field（词汇场）：一系列相关的词汇。例如，食物与饮料。

Objective（目标）：老师希望学生运用在课上学到的知识点在课后完成的任务。例如，运用目标语言写一张贺卡。

Pair-work/group-work（二人/小组联系）：学生共同完成老师布置的活动或任务。

Personalisation（个性化）：老师根据学生需要和课堂气氛灵活运用课堂练习，教材中的活动和素材。

Picture dictation（听画）：学生画出老师或其他学生描述的事物。口述的人通常先描述整个场景，然后分一到两次用短语或句子表述出这件事物。

Prescription v description（指示对描述）：在交际语言课上，描述而不是指示规则被认为是一种好的教学方法。例如，"have" 在 *I have been to Beijing twice.* 这句话中是助动词，但是在"*I have two brothers, a sister and a dog called Deng.*"中是"拥有"的意思。

Practice（练习）：学生运用角色扮演，信息隔阂和问卷调查等方式有意义地练习学到的语言点。（见表 7）

Procedure（步骤）：老师将一节课付诸实施的步骤。

Product（产品）：一项活动的的物质产出。例如，在一节写作课上写给国外朋友的一张贺卡。

Production（生产）：通过让学生以最自由的方法运用目标结构来培养他们更好的使用目标语言的能力。

Recycling（回收）：老师在一节课的练习或生产阶段再次引入过去学过的语法或词汇。

Role play（角色扮演）：学生根据情景扮演其中的角色。例如，一位顾客与一位服务员在饭店，或第一次约会（见 The Wallflowers）。

Skimming（略读）：以要点或主旨为目的的快速阅读法。例如，这篇文章是关于谁的？

Scanning（浏览）：以特定信息为目的的快速阅读法。例如，第七行的这个单词是什么意思？(a) ----- (b) ----- (c) ----- (d) -----

Signposting（指路标）：给学生们明确指出这节课中正在练习的内容。例如，给这节课一个标题。（见表 5）

Stage（阶段）：一节课中的一部分。例如，阶段（1）对与服装有关的词汇进行头脑风暴；阶段（2）与另一对或一组交换想到的单词。

Sentence stress（句重音）：一句话中强调的音节。（见表 1）

Student needs（学生需要）：学生在一节课或一个课程中需要理解的知识点。通常由课程教学大纲决定。

Target structure（目标结构）：一节课中作为重点的语法结构。例如，在讲解不规则过去式变换的课上使用这样的句式：*Yesterday Shen went to the seaside. He didn't go to the ice cream shop, but he swam in the sea with the dolphins.*

Task（任务）：一项由老师设定，学生完成的活动。通常包括一个小作业。例如，与你的搭档合作想出 10 个以"s"开头的单词，时间 5 分钟，至少找到 20 个。

Timing（定时）：老师给一项活动分配的时间。

Warmer（热身）：让学生热身并进入学习状态的 5 分钟小活动。例如，猜字游戏。

Word diamond（词钻）：以钻石的形状将文章中的单词被写在黑板上。（见表 5）

Word stress（词重音）：一个单词通常可以被划分为几个重音。为方便教学，重音通常以■ 或重音符标记。（见表 5)

Images and Photos

The images in this book have been created from digital photos either held in the public domain or under Creative Commons Attribution Share Alike licenses. Peter and Paul would like to express their enthusiasm and appreciation of all those who donate their work to Creative Commons and whose work is celebrated here.

The following licenses are referred to in the notes below:

CCO 1.0: Universal Public Domain Dedication
(www. creativecommons.org/public domain/zero/1.0/legalcode)
CC BY-SA 2.0: Attribution Share Alike Generic
(www. creativecommons.org/licenses/by-sa/2.0/legalcode)
CC BY-SA 2.5: Attribution Share Alike Generic
(www. creativecommons.org/licenses/by-sa/2.5/legalcode)
CC BY-SA 3.0: Attribution Share Alike Unported
(www. creativecommons.org/licenses/by-sa/3.0/legalcode)
CC BY-SA 4.0: Attribution Share Alike International
(www. creativecommons.org/licenses/by-sa/4.0/legalcode)

(1) Cover design, derivative of two profiles, royalty free image from dreamtime stock photos by S Proctor. Scaled and overlaid from original. Text added by authors.
(2) Thalia, derivative of illustration of Nine Muses (1832) by Samuel Griswold Goodrich, public domain. Cropped, scaled and overlaid from original with border.
(3) Peter and Paul, derivative of Tony Head Shot and Sedley Head Shot by Rockdraw. Scaled and overlaid from original with border.
(4) Neighbour's Clogs, derivative of woman at her toilet (1659-60) by Jan Steen, public domain. Scaled and overlaid from original with border.
(5) Very Bad, derivative of "Bad Girls" (1958) by James Meese, public domain. Scaled and overlaid from original with border.
(6) The Emperor and the Scribe, derivative of Pereginus, Pompeii inscription by Fer.filol, public domain. Scaled and overlaid from original with border. Text added by authors.
(7) The Wall Flowers, derivative of a romantic kiss on Greek beach at sunset (2010) by Scarleth White under CC BY-SA 2.0. Scaled and overlaid from original with border.
(8) Dust and Drapery, derivative of illustration of Laclos' *Dangerous Liaisons:* Letter 71 *Valmont enfonçant la porte de la Vicomtesse* (1796) by Charles Monnet, public domain. Scaled and overlaid from original with border.
(9) Very Good, derivative of sexy kissable red lips, happy girl (2012) by Robert & Michaela Vicol, public domain. Scaled and overlaid from original with border.
(10) The Snake, derivative of portrait of Giulia Leonardi (ca 1910) by Ferdinand Hodler, public domain. Scaled and overlaid from original with border.

Lightning Source UK Ltd.
Milton Keynes UK
UKOW07f0422100117

291755UK00002B/7/P